The Case of the Missing Baseball Glove!

SHARA PUGLISI KATSOS

Illustrated by
John Bulens

A portion of the sales of this book will be donated to PAWS New England

Visit us on Facebook at
www.facebook.com/Doggie.Investigation.Gang

Copyright 2017 by Shara Puglisi Katsos
Doggie Investigation Gang, DIG ™ 2017
By Shara Puglisi Katsos
Published by Katman Productions, LLC
Illustrated by John Bulens
Edited by Tanya Gold
ISBN 978-1-5323-3276-0

Printed in the United States of America

March 2017

This book is dedicated to our
blue-eyed beagle friend, Gizmo.
You will live on in our hearts and
in the imaginations of children for
a long time to come.

Contents

Introduction

"I lost my baseball glove," cried Jacob. "I can't find it anywhere."

With tears streaming down his reddened cheeks, seven-year-old Jacob ran and hugged his parents. Looking up at their faces, he said, "I don't know where it could be. I can't play in my team's baseball game tomorrow without it. It's my lucky glove!"

Jacob's parents tried to reassure him that they would find it before his baseball game. They said that if they couldn't find it in time, they could borrow one from his coach or buy a new one.

"I don't want a new one. That one is special. It was from Grampy," cried Jacob.

His parents looked to one another with hopes that the glove would be found.

Sunbathing

"Did you hear that, Lily?" shouted Rocky.

Rocky and Lily were two small, white poodle siblings that lived in a house beside Jacob's. Rocky loved to play with Jacob and considered him a dear friend.

"Did I hear what?" Lily asked calmly as she was lying on her lounge chair on the sun porch. "Why are you making such a fuss on this quiet Saturday morning? Mom and Dad built me this beautiful sun porch so that I can relax. I let you sit with me and all you do is talk, talk, talk. And the neighbors are so noisy, too. How can I relax with all this noise?"

"They built the sun porch for both of us, Lily. Daddy even told me so," Rocky replied, rolling his eyes at Lily. "Anyway, Jacob lost his baseball glove. He's heartbroken. I have never seen him cry before. I feel so sad for him."

"Well, if you feel so bad for him, why don't you do something about it?" Lily said with snootiness in her voice.

"You're right, Lily!" Rocky replied with delight. "I have an idea of who can help!"

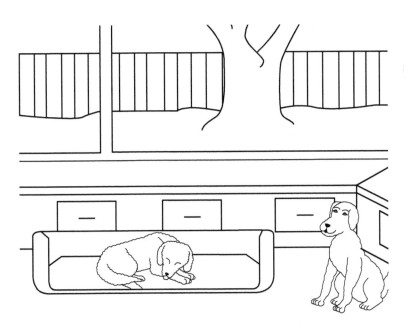

2

A Flying Friend

As the members of the Doggie Investigation Gang were relaxing outside by the pool in the back yard, a delicate, grey bird swooped overhead and swiftly landed on the pool gate.

"Are you the Doggie Investigation Gang?" asked the little bird sweetly. She was small and thin with a black beak and a distinct red patch under her tail.

"Who said that?" asked Pedro.

"You must be Pedro!" replied the bird with delight.

"I am," said Pedro proudly.

"I knew it," said the bird. "I was told that you are blind and have an amazing sense of smell. And that Cooper is clever. And that Charlie can tell time."

"Oh boy," said Charlie. "I can't tell time. I just don't like to be late for anything. Can you imagine if I could tell time though? I would be on time for all my meals. Wow, that would be so great."

"Who are you?" asked Cooper. "I have never talked to a bird before."

"How inconsiderate of me. Let me introduce myself. My name is Chloe. I'm a catbird," she said cheerfully.

"A mutual friend of ours, Rocky, asked me to come see you. He told me about how you work together to solve mysteries."

Chloe flew a little closer to the gang. "Rocky and I have been friends for many years. He tells me the stories of your past adventures while I eat my breakfast from a bird feeder in his yard. While I was eating my breakfast this morning, he asked me to bring you a message."

"Rocky lives with our grammy, grandpa and Lily. You flew all this way? The message must be important," said Charlie.

"It is important. There's a boy named Jacob that lives in a house beside Rocky's and he's been crying all day. It seems that he lost his baseball glove. He's devastated because the glove was a gift from his grampy and he needs it for tomorrow's baseball game.

"A gift from his grampy. That does sound special," Pedro said. "I feel bad for him. It sounds like the glove means a lot to him. We must help him."

"I agree," replied Charlie.

"We need to get to our grammy and grandpa's house," answered Cooper.

"Oh dear. Travel? How will we do that?" asked Charlie.

"Here's the plan!" shouted Cooper, wagging his labrador tail with excitement.

3

Grammy and Grandpa's House

In the early evening, Cooper, Charlie and Pedro did exactly as Cooper had planned. They ran around the house and jumped up and down in front of their mom.

"What has gotten into you three today? My goodness you have a lot of energy. Do you need to do something fun today to help burn off some of that energy? Let's see, do you want to go to Bow Wow Park?"

Cooper, Charlie and Pedro just sat still and stared at her.

"Hmm, that's not it," said their mom. "Do you want to go to Lickadee Lake?"

All three dogs continued to sit as still as can be.

"Hmm, do you want to go to grammy and grandpa's to visit Rocky and Lily?"

The Doggie Investigation Gang jumped up and down with approval.

"Okay, said their mom, let me get my keys and we can go."

"That was easy," said Pedro.

"Mom can be pretty smart," said Charlie.

Cooper rolled his eyes, thinking it was his smart plan all along.

"Okay, fine, Cooper, that was a smart idea," said Charlie.

The Interview

While their mom drove to their grammy and grandpa's house, Cooper, Charlie and Pedro quietly shared their excitement with one another.

"It is so fun to be on another adventure," said Pedro excitedly.

"Yes, it is," said Cooper.

"Especially when it takes us to Grammy and Grandpa's house. They love to feed us treats! Charlie replied.

As the vehicle pulled up the driveway, Lily and Rocky could see the car from the window.

Chloe had returned to her home in a cherry tree above Rocky's house. She was sitting on her favorite branch of the tree, looking down at Rocky's driveway, proud that she was able to help her friend.

"I can't believe it," said Rocky excitedly. "They're here! They're here! Chloe did it!"

"So they are," said Lily as she held her paw to her face to study her nails, trying to hide her concern.

After Cooper, Charlie and Pedro were greeted by their grandparents with treats and hugs, Rocky led the Doggie Investigation Gang to the porch. Lily followed out of curiosity. Rocky filled the gang in on the mystery while Chloe sat outside the porch screen door.

"As you can understand, Jacob is upset. His baseball glove was a gift from his grampy."

"We will find it," said Cooper.

"Yes, we will!" shouted Pedro. "We can do it!"

"It sounds special, we must find it!" exclaimed Charlie.

"I would be happy to help too," said Chloe.

"Wow! We've never had a bird on our team before! This is promising," said Charlie.

"Can you tell us anything more, Rocky?" Pedro asked inquisitively.

"When was the last time you noticed Jacob with his glove?"

Rocky tilted his head and squinted his eyes. He concentrated hard on the last time he noticed Jacob with his baseball glove and ball. "It was yesterday," he exclaimed. "The last time I saw his baseball mitt it was hanging off the handlebars of Jacob's red shiny bike. It was early evening and the sun was getting low in the sky as the evening breeze was beginning to cool the summer night. I remember noticing that the breeze had pushed his bike over and it fell to the ground."

"Stupendous!" cried Pedro in excitement. "We are making progress now."

"Please proceed," Charlie calmly requested while looking at Rocky with thoughtful eyes. "Did the baseball glove slide off the handlebars?"

"Hmmm," replied Rocky. "I can't remember. I was beginning to doze off at the time."

"Try to visualize what happened, Rocky," said Cooper.

"I remember! It stayed on the handlebars! That's right."

"Outstanding!" exclaimed Pedro.

"Lily is there anything that you observed yesterday that may be able to assist us in finding the glove?" asked Charlie.

Lily, who was lying on her back with her paws up admiring her newly manicured nails throughout the entire conversation, replied in a disinterested tone, "That sounds accurate to me."

"We are very grateful for your assistance, Rocky. Now we know where to begin our investigation, which is in Jacob's yard," announced Cooper.

Pedro Power

As the evening drew near, the Doggie Investigation Gang went into their grandparents back yard. Cooper quickly located a small opening in the fence to Jacob's yard. After looking around and making some quick calculations, Cooper knew there was only one dog that could master this part of the investigation, Pedro.

"Pedro, you're the only one of us that can fit through the gap in the fence. You're just the right size to venture through to Jacob's yard. Can you do it alone?" asked Cooper.

"Yes, I can do it!" Pedro replied proudly.

"I will follow you from the sky," said Chloe.

"And Charlie and I will stay right here. Just shout out to us if you need any us," said Cooper.

Pedro was excited to be involved in an investigation again, and with the support of a bird! He was ready for the challenge.

As he passed through the fence opening, he could hear Chloe's little wings flapping above him. He felt a thrill of excitement and suspense through his little body.

He walked carefully around the yard, relying on his sense of smell to find important clues. He thought of when his human friend Luke had played catch with him and how the glove had smelled of old leather.

As Pedro was thinking back on this fond memory and the smell of the glove, he found a clue!

The Tomato Garden

Pedro smelled something similar to his past experience with a baseball glove. He remembered the old leather smell. With his nose touching the grass, he moved swiftly through the yard, following the scent.

Suddenly, Chloe yelled down to him, "I see it, Pedro! It's Jacob's bike. It's still lying on the ground where the summer wind had blew it over, just as Rocky said."

"Good work. Gracias, Chloe!"

Pedro continued walking steadily. His four little paws moved faster as he became more and more excited, knowing that he was near the answer to their investigation.

"Be careful, Pedro!" yelled Chloe at the top of her little bird lungs.

And, just as Pedro was about to run into a tomato plant, he stopped. "Thanks Chloe!" he exclaimed as he rubbed his forehead with one of his front paws. "My excitement got the best of me!"

"Everything all right?" yelled Charlie from the other side of the fence.

"Yes!" Pedro yelled back with excitement. "I just found the baseball glove! And it's buried in a tomato garden!"

Pedro dug between the tomato plants as quickly as he could until he reached the glove. He lifted it gently with his teeth so he didn't rip it. He knew how much it meant to Jacob.

Pedro boldly made his way back to Cooper and Charlie with his new friend Chloe flying above. He went through Jacob's yard and through the small opening in the fence. He pushed the mitt through the opening with his nose and gave it to Cooper.

"Magnificent!" shouted Charlie. "Your nose really is amazing!"

Pedro was proud and happy. He had been feeling badly for Jacob since hearing about his lost baseball glove.

"We solved the case!" shouted Chloe.

"Actually," whispered Cooper to Charlie and Pedro, "there is still one more mystery. Why was the baseball mitt buried in the tomato garden?"

"Wait a minute," replied Charlie. "Did you notice that Lily was examining her nails for a long time? She had just had them manicured. And she was not very helpful when we asked her questions."

"That's typical of Lily though. She's always admiring herself," said Cooper.

"That is true, Cooper, but it looked like she had just been to the groomer," Charlie replied.

"You think Lily buried the glove, and Grammy and Grandpa had to take her to the groomer because she was dirty from the garden?" asked Pedro with disappointment in his voice.

"Just a thought," replied Charlie.

"You are an intelligent and observant spaniel, Charlie," Cooper said.

Pedro nodded in agreement.

"Let's go ask Lily a few questions," said Pedro boldly.

Remorse

Cooper, Charlie and Pedro found Rocky and Lily resting on the back porch.

"Pedro found the baseball glove," Charlie informed them.

"That's incredible!" Rocky yelled with happiness and relief in his voice. "I knew you could do it! That was fast too. I cannot wait for Jacob to find out. He will be so thrilled!"

"You what?" Lily asked with a hint of guilt in her voice. "You found the glove? Where?"

"It was buried in his parent's tomato garden," replied Cooper.

"Who would do that?" questioned Rocky sadly. "That's not very nice. Everyone knows how much Jacob loves his glove."

"Lily, do you want to tell Rocky or should we?" asked Charlie.

"How did you know it was me?" Lily replied, looking guilty and sad.

"We had an idea that it was you, but you just confirmed it," Cooper stated.

"Yes, it was me. It's just that every night, while I am resting on our back porch, I can hear Jacob making so much noise in the back yard. I can't relax with all that noise. And, sometimes Rocky is out there playing with him and I can hear them having so much fun with Rocky happily barking and Jacob cheering." She let out a big sigh and looked at the floor.

"Do you want to play with Jacob and me?" asked Rocky sympathetically. "I never thought to ask you before, because you never seemed interested in what I like to do."

"Of course I'm interested. Rocky, you're my brother."

"Lily, I'm so sorry. You can play with us any time!" replied Rocky.

"Thanks Rocky," she said before continuing to tell Rocky, the Doggie Investigation Gang and Chloe what had happened the other night. "Like Rocky said, the wind blew the bike over with the baseball glove on the handlebars. And I thought that was my opportunity. I quietly went through the fence, took the mitt and buried it," she said quietly. "Honestly, I did not realize how sad Jacob would be when it was gone. I thought I would get a few days of peace and quiet before his parents bought him a new one. And then, when I saw how sad he was, I felt badly."

"How come you didn't help us when we were asking you questions?" Pedro asked with empathy and intrigue in his voice.

"I guess I was embarrassed and I was hoping you would find it, but you wouldn't know who did it," Lily confessed.

"You underestimated the Doggie Investigation Gang, Lily!" yelled

Rocky, a disappointed tone in his voice.

"I know," replied Lily quietly, looking at the ground. "I do feel terrible."

Cooper, Charlie and Pedro huddled to discuss what to do next. Cooper had an idea!

32

Joy

Jacob was in his driveway, sitting
on his bicycle and looking very sad

when his parents came out to tell him it was time to leave for his game.

"I don't want to go," replied Jacob.

"Don't you want to cheer on your team?"

"Not really," Jacob replied.

And, as he was about to cry, Lily walked through the hole in the fence with his glove held gently in her mouth. She walked up to him and dropped it at his feet.

"My glove!" yelled Jacob with joy. "Thank you, thank you, thank you, Lily!" He ran circles around his parents and Lily in pure delight. "Let's get to the baseball field!"

Since Lily could not apologize verbally to Jacob, as people do not understand dog language, she licked his hand.

Inside, her heart was smiling. She had been feeling badly and now she felt better for doing the right thing. She was thrilled to see Jacob happy again.

The Next Adventure

Cooper, Charlie and Pedro were back home, sitting on their deck.

"I really wish we could have seen Jacob's face and hear his excitement when Lily returned his glove," said Charlie.

"I know," said Cooper.

Just then, their new friend Chloe flew by and sat on the deck railing.

"I thought you might want to hear all about Jacob's reunion with his glove!" she shouted from her stoop.

"Yes, indeed," replied Pedro.

"He was so thrilled. He gave Lily the biggest hug and then he hugged his parents and ran to their car in a hurry. He was happier than a kid on Christmas morning."

The Doggie Investigation Gang was happy to hear the good news. They were proud of Lily for doing the right thing.

"And Lily," Charlie asked with concern in his voice, "was she okay?"

"She was beaming with happiness from ear to tail," replied Chloe. "And, Rocky is planning to invite her to play catch with him and Jacob later today."

"Good for Lily!" Pedro twirled happily. "I just love happy endings!"

"What's next?" Chloe continued. "Need any assistance on your next adventure?"

"We were thinking of taking some time to relax and enjoy the summer weather," said Cooper.

And just as he finished his sentence, Cooper, Charlie, Pedro and Chloe heard a cry from the second floor of the Doggie Investigation Gang's house.

"My tutu! It's gone!" cried Sophie, their little human toddler.

"Don't go too far, Chloe. We just might," Cooper replied.

With mixed emotions of excitement for a new mystery and sadness to hear Sophie upset, the Doggie Investigation Gang jumped up from their resting positions ready to help their Sophie find her favorite tutu.

The End

About the Pups

Cooper is a yellow labrador retriever. He has a knack for adventure and enjoys swimming and playing catch with his family. Cooper is a certified therapy dog who has been known to visit Veterans at nearby Veterans Administration Hospitals. He enjoys meeting America's heroes and thanking them for their service.

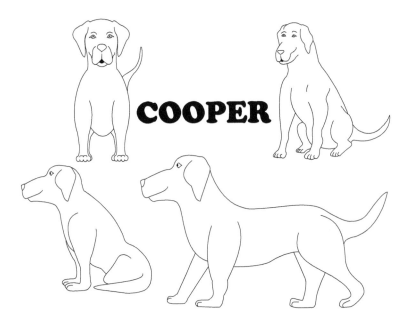

COOPER

Charlie is a cocker spaniel. His hobbies include walking and swimming. He enjoys hanging out and watching movies with his family. Charlie is also a certified therapy dog who enjoys new people to love and cuddle.

CHARLIE

Pedro is a minpin. He was rescued by PAWS New England from a puppy mill. As a result of his experience in a puppy mill he has glaucoma, which has resulted in his blindness. Pedro does not let his blindness hinder him from enjoying his new life with his adoptive family, which includes his two brothers, Cooper and Charlie.

PEDRO

Lily is a white poodle. Lily was adopted when she was 18 months old. She is a smart dog who knows about 10 to 15 human words. She enjoys treats, watching movies, having popcorn with her family, as well as day trips to the park.

Rocky is a white poodle/shih tzu mix. He was adopted when he was 7 years old. He enjoys walking, relaxing and finding a warm sunny spot to take long naps. If he likes you, he will roll onto his back so that you can give him a belly rub.

About the Author

Shara Katsos has a Master of Social Work degree and is a licensed independent social worker who is employed at the Veterans Healthcare Administration (VHA). Her hobbies include spending time with her husband, Steve, their daughter, Sophie, and the Doggie Investigation Gang.

About the Illustrators

John Bulens has a Bachelor of Art in Philosophy and a Certificate in Graphic Design. He has been freelancing in graphic design and desktop layout for a number of years. In addition, he enjoys volunteering for an international television show that highlights local artists and comedians. He is a close friend of the members of the Doggie Investigation Gang.

Robert Comora is the creator of the DIG badge. He is also an advocate for the safety and well-being of dogs. He and his wife, Janet, have rescued two dogs of their own that have made special appearances in the Doggie Investigation Gang Book Series.

A Note to the Grown Up(s)

Thank you for your purchase of the third story in the Doggie Investigation Gang, DIG Book Series. A portion of all sales of this book will be donated to PAWS New England – All Breed Dog Rescue.

PAWS New England rescues abandoned, neglected, and abused dogs. In addition, they educate the community of the importance of spay-and-neuter programs to help control the dog population and stop the problem at its source.

Since PAWS New England has started they have saved the lives of more than 7,500 dogs.

To learn more about PAWS New England, adopt/foster a dog or make a donation, please visit their website at www.pawsnewengland.com.

Did you enjoy this story? Keep a look out for the Doggie Investigation Gang's next adventure:

The Case of the Missing Tutu!

Check us out on Facebook at
www.facebook.com/Doggie.Investiagtion.Gang

CPSIA information can be obtained
at www.ICGtesting.com
Printed in the USA
FSHW020601150619
59067FS